*For my brilliant nieces
Rebecca and Emma*

**Library and Archives Canada Cataloguing in Publication**

Cassidy, Sara, author
The Great Googlini / Sara Cassidy ; illustrated by Charlene Chua.
(Orca echoes)

Issued in print and electronic formats.
ISBN 978-1-4598-1703-6 (softcover).—ISBN 978-1-4598-1704-3 (PDF).—
ISBN 978-1-4598-1705-0 (EPUB)

I. Chua, Charlene, 1980–, illustrator  II. Title.  III. Series: Orca echoes

PS8555.A7812G74 2018          jC813'.54          C2017-907678-7
                              C2017-907679-5

First published in the United States, 2018
Library of Congress Control Number: 2018933730

**Summary**: In this chapter book, a young boy copes with his uncle's cancer diagnosis by seeking
answers from the Great Googlini, an information scientist who emerges from his computer.

Orca Book Publishers gratefully acknowledges the support for its publishing programs
provided by the following agencies: the Government of Canada through the Canada Book Fund
and the Canada Council for the Arts, and the Province of British Columbia
through the BC Arts Council and the Book Publishing Tax Credit.

Edited by Liz Kemp
Cover artwork and interior illustrations by Charlene Chua
Author photo by Amaya Tarasoff

ORCA BOOK PUBLISHERS
orcabook.com

Printed and bound in Canada.

21  20  19  18  •  4  3  2  1

# The Great Googlini

## Sara Cassidy

Illustrated by **Charlene Chua**

ORCA BOOK PUBLISHERS

## Chapter One

"I am coming to the end of my tenth orbit around the sun," I tell Ivan.

"You've traveled nearly nine billion four hundred million kilometers," Ivan says.

Ivan is super smart. And skinny, like stretched toffee. Me, I'm toffee before it got stretched—short and wide. Ivan and I have been best friends since kindergarten.

"How can traveling through space make me older? I mean, I can't even feel it."

"If you could, you'd have no skin," Ivan says. "Atmosphere burn. A lot worse than carpet burn."

We're in front of my mom's old computer, googling *salt* for a school project. We've watched cars race across the huge salt flats of Utah—they look like fields of snow—and have learned that Canadians put more salt on icy highways than they do on food.

Mrs. Zupan hands us steaming bowls of goulash through the window. "Here, boys."

Ivan takes a bite. "Pass the sodium chloride."

I hand him the saltshaker.

We stare at the screen again. The cursor flashes in the search bar, as if Google is tapping its toe: *Throw something at me. Anything.*

"Okay, Google," I say. The microphone throbs for input. "Google!"

Google churns and spits out the top results for Google.

It has found itself.

"Ha," Ivan says. "My turn. Okay, Google..."

But before he can speak, I sneeze.

*Ah-choo!*

Google hears *pet chip.*

So, as Ivan and I gobble our goulash, we learn about microchips the size of a grain of rice that you can get injected under your pet's skin. The chip has a code, so if the animal gets lost, the

chip company can figure out where it is. Dogs, cats, horses, snakes—even rare fish get microchip implants.

"Fish and chips!" I say.

"How could a fish get lost?" Ivan asks.

Ivan is smart about smart things but not about normal things.

"They get stolen, not lost. Some koi are worth more than a car."

Just then Ivan's father's car rattles into the parking lot down below.

"Definitely more than *that* car," I add.

Ivan's car is held together with bungee cords. Ivan's dad honks. Ivan grabs his backpack. "Thank Mrs. Zupan for the galoshes. And don't forget to invite me to your orbit-completion celebration."

I snort. Who else would I invite to my birthday party?

I spend another hour at the computer. I get sucked in. The screen is basically a window showing the whole world. The windows of our apartment only show the buildings next door.

# Chapter Two

Our apartment building is like a brown shoe box. It's squeezed between other brown shoe boxes on Third Street East. The town's name is Bording. It's a clump of low buildings stuck to the edge of the big city. Like a growth.

Bording is named after a pretty town in England. I looked it up on Google Street View. Bording in England has narrow streets, stone houses and cute, roundish cars. Bording in British Columbia is *not* pretty. Sometimes a sparrow looks cute, pecking at the dirt in the sidewalk cracks, and in spring cherry petals flutter in the breeze like snow. But mostly, Bording is dull. My uncles don't even pronounce the *d*. "How do people stay awake in Boring?" they ask.

Uncle Mato and Uncle Boris live forty minutes away in Vancouver, where there are mansions and skyscrapers and the grocery stores sell twenty types of salt—lilac salt, bacon salt, Himalayan pink salt, black truffle Italian sea salt, even chocolate salt. Here in Bording you get one kind of salt—salt.

I'm still at the computer when the building's ancient elevator rumbles and its doors screech open. Mom's home! I've been at the screen for more than the two hours I'm allowed each day. I put the computer in sleep mode, dive onto the couch, stretch out my legs and open a magazine, all in one move.

Mom comes through the door. "Hi, dear."

"Hi," I answer, trying not to sound out of breath.

"You're reading about the sales?" Mom asks, surprised.

The "magazine" is actually the flyer for the local supermarket.

"Yep."

Mom shrugs. "Circle anything that you want for your birthday."

Mom is nice. Dad is nice too. I don't have any brothers or sisters, only a salamander named Hitokage. That's the Japanese name for Charmander from Pokémon.

Mom and Dad own The Paprenjak, a coffee shop on Main Street with big tables and fluorescent lights that hum and tick. A *paprenjak* is like a gingerbread cookie, but more peppery. People eat it in Croatia. Croatia is across the Adriatic Sea from Italy, and it's where Mom and Dad are from. They immigrated to Canada because it was too hard to find work there. My dad's brothers, Uncle Boris and Uncle Mato— he's my favorite—came with them. Mom was pregnant with me when they boarded the plane.

"You were a world traveler before you were born" she likes to tell me.

How did I start? Like a seed in a garden. Planted the moment Mom and Dad first saw each other in a dark, noisy nightclub in Zagreb. Ten years ago.

A decade. The word, Google tells me, comes from *deka*, ancient Greek for ten. As in *deca*pods—lobsters, crabs, shrimp and other creatures that crawl through life on ten legs.

Ten. As in my ten toes, which Mom says she counted the day I was born, to make sure all of me had arrived.

Ten. The Chinese write +. The Romans wrote X. In English we make a one and a zero, a stick and a stone, a French fry beside an onion ring, 1-0. Like binary code, the computer's heartbeat.

# Chapter Three

I say there's Mom, Dad, Uncle Mato and Uncle Boris in my family. But there's also Mrs. Zupan, who is also from Croatia. Her apartment is in the shoe box next to ours, in a whole other building, but it's like she's in the next room. It's like she lives with us. Our kitchen window looks into her kitchen window, a meter away. I once stretched a broom handle across the distance, marked it with a

piece of chalk, then used a ruler to get
the measure.

When we moved into our sixth-floor
apartment, Mrs. Zupan was at her stove,
stirring stew, a cloud of steam billowing
out her window and into ours. Mom and

Dad stopped in their tracks and forgot the heavy boxes in their arms.

"*Janjetina*!" Mom sighed.

Dad closed his eyes. "Janjetina," he swooned. They were in a trance. Janjetina, I now know, is roast lamb with paprika, sour cream and parsley. It's a favorite meal in Croatia.

Mrs. Zupan put down her wooden spoon, and we all shook hands across the gap between the buildings. An hour later she handed a pot of janjetina through the window. Janjetina was our first meal in our new apartment.

A long time ago Ivan and I dropped a ball out the kitchen window and counted the seconds—*one chimpanzee, two chim*—until it hit the grass. We timed the fall with the clock on Ivan's iPod too. For both measurements we got a second and a half. Ivan did the math. Objects fall at nine meters per second, so the drop was about thirteen meters.

But Ivan wanted an exact measurement. So we tied a bolt to the end of my mom's roll of parcel string and lowered it to the ground—13.3 meters. According to Google, that's the length of the neck of an *Apatosaurus*. We now call the gap between the buildings the Apatosaurus Chasm.

At the bottom is a strip of pale grass that no one bothers to water. The worms I get there for Hitokage—when I can't find them anywhere else—are thin. But on sunny days in early summer the grass is green and high and dotted with yellow dandelions. It reminds Mom of a field in Croatia that she played in as a girl.

When we first moved in, Mrs. Zupan told us that cooking—frying onions for *burek* or roasting red peppers for *ajvar*—cheered her up. Her husband had just died, she said, and cooking gave her something to do. "It's better than crying."

I was only six then and felt terrible, hearing about her husband. "Don't worry, Filip," she said to me. "Life is a beautiful flower. Once in a while, though, it must be watered with tears."

Mrs. Zupan did so much cooking that her fridge and freezer filled up. Uncle Boris, who is huge and strong, helped Dad move a second freezer into Mrs. Zupan's apartment. There was so little room in the elevator, they sat on the freezer for the ride up.

Then *that* freezer filled up, and Mrs. Zupan started handing platters of

cabbage rolls and shish kabobs across
Apatosaurus Chasm to us, for supper,
lunch, breakfast! Finally Dad asked Mrs.
Zupan if she would like to cook for The
Paprenjak. People come all the way from
Vancouver for her meals.

Often while I'm tapping—*tap-
tap*—on the keyboard, Mrs. Zupan's
chopping at her cutting board—*chop-
chop*. Garlic, potatoes, parsley, turnips.
Once in a while she asks me to google the
weather report for the village where she
grew up, or home remedies for arthritis.
Sometimes she shouts to me to find an
online Croatian radio station. I turn up
the volume, and she whirls around her
kitchen to the accordion music.

# Chapter Four

Every Wednesday, Uncle Mato drives up from Vancouver and I meet him at The Paprenjak after school. I have a cup of chocolate milk and we head to the soccer field. But this week when I arrive at the coffeehouse, things feel different. Uncle Mato, Mom and Dad are at a table drinking coffee as usual, but when I push open the door, making the bell jump on its string, my family doesn't greet me

with noisy, teasing hellos. Instead they clam up and stare.

"What did I do?" I ask. "Hello-o?"

Uncle Mato hops up. "Okay, okay. We were talking about your birthday present. The fact is, you aren't getting anything."

"Maybe—a lump of coal," Dad says.

"Coal is a Christmas thing, Dad." After ten years in Canada, my parents still get things confused. Dad once lit fireworks on Thanksgiving, and Mom has served turkey with cranberry sauce on Canada Day.

"Right," Uncle Mato says. "Then you're not even getting coal."

Dad nods stiffly. He looks pale. Mom too. "It's true, son," Dad says. "We've got nothing for you."

Dad's a terrible liar. But last night he and Mom *were* sorting through the bills and grumbling.

Mom can't stand it. "They're joking, Filip. They're meanos."

"It's *meanies*, not *meanos*," I say.

I'm glad it was a joke, but it wasn't funny. My knees feel like oatmeal.

Uncle Mato gives me one of his bear hugs, then lifts me over his head until I touch the ceiling. We've done this since I was little. My handprints are all over the place up there. The smallest are the darkest—chocolate pudding and mud puddle.

Uncle Mato gets the soccer ball from his bag.

"You're playing?" Mom asks. "Today?"

"Why wouldn't we?" I ask.

"The weather's not so good."

"Are you crazy?"

"Filip," Dad warns.

"Worry pimple," Uncle Mato teases
Mom, smiling. Uncle Mato has beautiful,
sparkly teeth. Everyone says so.

Mom's eyes tear up.

"Mom, he's just teasing!"

Soon Uncle Mato and I are leaping along the sidewalk's graham-cracker slabs, trying to touch each square once only. It's easier for Uncle Mato since his legs are longer than mine. I trot after him.

"Well, Filip," Uncle Mato says. "You're at the end of the single digits. Once you cross into the land of double digits, there's no going back."

"I know," I pant. An airplane chalks a dusty line across the blue sky. "But I can't not enter the land of the double digits."

"True." Uncle Mato slows down. We're at the soccer park.

"Anyway, I'm aiming for three digits."

Uncle Mato ruffles my hair. "Why not shoot for four, like Tom Bombadil in *Lord of the Rings*?"

"That would be so cool," I say, imagining being over a thousand years old.

"You could sing trees to sleep, like he does."

I laugh. Nothing that exciting would ever happen to me. Hopping up Main Street with Uncle Mato on Wednesday afternoons is as exciting as my life gets.

While Uncle Mato tightens his shoelaces, I ask him The Question. I ask it every week. For a year the answer has been no.

"So. Do you have a girlfriend?"

"Pardon?"

"You know what I said. Do you have a girlfriend?"

"I can't hear you."

I put my hands on my hips and shout, "DO YOU HAVE A GIRLFRIEND?!"

"As a matter of fact, yes."

"*Yes*?" I jump on Uncle Mato's back.

"Sort of."

"Sort of?"

"Nearly."

"*Who*?"

"A nurse."

"In white shoes with rubbery soles?"

"When she's at work, yes." Uncle Mato lowers me to the ground.

"Where did you meet?"

"The hospital."

"What were you doing at a hospital?"

"Uh…just wandering around."

"People don't just wander around hospitals."

"You're right." Uncle Mato's giant eyebrow ripples. The eyebrow is thick and black and runs over both of his eyes without breaking at his nose. It thins a little there, but basically Uncle Mato has one eyebrow. If you look at it too long, it starts to wiggle like a tropical millipede. Sometimes I've worried that Uncle Mato's eyebrow was why he couldn't get a girlfriend.

"I was visiting a friend." He shrugs.

He dropkicks the soccer ball. The ball hits a tree trunk, sending a batch of crows squawking from the branches into the sky. Then, without touching the ground, the ball flies toward a power pole. It bounces off the power pole and then—incredible!—zooms directly into the soccer net. *Zing, bong, whoosh!*

"Goal!" Uncle Mato shouts. "Ludicrous goal!"

We burst out laughing and end up rolling on the ground, holding our stomachs, trying to catch our breath.

Finally I wipe my eyes and stare up at the blue sky, where the crows are still flapping around.

Each crow looks like Uncle Mato's eyebrow.

# Chapter Five

"...and today is Filip Horvat's birthday."

Through the PA speaker, the principal sounds like a robot with a head cold. "Filip, to the office!"

Nearly every day a student gets called down for a birthday surprise. Stuck at your desk, you hear the lucky kid scurry down the empty hallway like a spirit. Today I'm the one scurrying down the hallway. *I'm* the birthday ghost.

Principal Jansen steps off her treadmill. "Happy birthday, Filip," she says, patting at her neck with a towel. "Ten's a big year."

Last year she said *nine's a big year*. And the year before that, *eight's a big year*.

"Are any years small?" I ask.

Principal Jansen squashes her nose with her forefinger. After a moment she lifts her finger, and her nose springs back into place. "Yes. Fifty-three is pretty small. Fifty-four might be too, but I don't know for sure yet."

She opens the "birthday chest," which is really just the bottom drawer of her filing cabinet, decorated with pink ribbons. "Do you still like dinosaurs?"

"They're all right."

I've been reaching into the surprise chest since kindergarten. Back then

I'd yank the drawer open without even saying hello. By third grade I'd learned to wait until the drawer was open *and* Principal Jansen was out of the way. Now I don't even look as she opens the drawer. Instead I watch two seagulls fight over a forgotten lunch bag in the schoolyard. They tear the bag open, and Goldfish crackers spray into the wood chips. Fish and chips!

It's not that I'm less excited about the birthday surprise. I've just learned not to *look* excited. Fifth-graders don't jump up and down. But *inside* I'm jumping up and down.

Principal Jansen nudges me toward the drawer. "Take a look."

Wind-up cars, paratroopers, finger traps, snap bracelets. I put in a hand and rummage gently. No dinosaurs. I plunge farther in and pull up a handful from the depths. Two dinosaurs! But the wrong kind. I get my second hand involved and bulldoze double scoops, sifting the toys through my fingers.

"Looking for anything in particular?"

"Nah," I say, churning through the toys.

I pull on the handle to see if the drawer opens any farther. There's a rumor

that there are still full-size chocolate bars at the very back, left over from the last principal. But I'm not looking for those. I pull up another giant fistful of toys. One toy bounces out and under Principal Jansen's desk. I peer into the darkness.

There it is, enveloped in a dust cloud, stubby legs in the air—the elusive *Stegosaurus*. The holy grail. I get on my belly and reach. I wiggle my fingertips, stick out my tongue.

I get it! I worm out from under the desk, coming up too early and bumping my head. The noise is huge.

I'm sweaty, my head is pounding, and the front of my shirt is brown with floor dirt.

"So that toy is okay?" Principal Jansen asks.

"Yeah, it's okay." I shrug. I'm clinging to the *Stegosaurus* so hard its plates dig into my hand.

"Have a big year, Filip."

# Chapter Six

Every year Mom forces me to have a birthday party. I've tried pouting, crying, kicking things—the works—but she has never backed down. On Wednesday, while Uncle Mato and I kicked the soccer ball back and forth, I told him I really, really, really, *really* didn't want to have a bunch of kids over.

"I heard you at the first *really*," he said.

Uncle Mato suggested "peace negotiations." An hour later Mom and I faced each other across a table at The Paprenjak while Uncle Mato, calling himself an "arbitrator," jotted notes on a napkin.

"I don't get a lot of chances to throw a birthday party," Mom protested. "I've only got one kid. You."

"Throw a party for Dad. Or for yourself," I said.

Mom shook her head. "Adults are no fun. Anyway, what kind of mom doesn't throw a birthday party for her beloved child?"

"A mom whose kid doesn't want to have a birthday party."

Uncle Mato wrote furiously on the napkin. He wagged his marker. "Filip, here's the thing. Your mother wants to do something nice for you."

"She always does nice things for me."

Mom fluttered. "I do?" She smiled. "Well, I try to." Then her eyes hardened. "Listen, if you don't have a birthday party, the other kids won't invite you to theirs."

"Awesome!"

Uncle Mato translated. "Sister, Filip isn't interested in attending other children's birthday parties."

Mom tried a different angle. "You'll hurt people's feelings by not inviting them to your party."

"But there's no party that I'm not inviting them to."

Uncle Mato drew a tick under *Logical Arguments*.

"Anyway," I said, "the only kid who cares—who *might* care—is Ivan."

Uncle Mato scribbled a few words, then multiple exclamation marks. "How about this?" he said. "You have a birthday party—"

Mom brightened.

"—with one guest. Ivan."

Mom bobbed her head, as if she was swishing the idea around in her brain.

"And your uncles."

"Yes," Mom decided. "That is okay with me."

"Filip?" Uncle Mato asked.

I didn't want to give in too quickly. "If I can have smoked sausage. And cheesy potato. And baklava."

"*Baklava?*" Mom asked. "Birthday candles stand up better in hot cross buns."

"Hot cross buns are for Easter."

"Right. Well, I'm not sure about baklava."

"The honey will hold the candles in place," Uncle Mato cooed, licking his lips. "You heard the part about the uncles being invited, right?"

# Chapter Seven

Ivan and I have a few hours to hang out before Uncle Mato, Uncle Boris and Uncle Boris's boyfriend, Kai, arrive for my birthday supper. We feed Hito her birthday bloodworms.

I got Hito for my birthday three years ago, which means our birthday is on the same day. Bloodworms are her standard birthday present. (I didn't realize Hito was a girl until a year after I named her.)

Normally she just gets earthworms from wherever I dig them up.

After that Ivan and I play *Minecraft*, then mess around on Google. When the uncles arrive, Kai shows us a few tricks created by Google programmers. If you type in *do a barrel roll*, the screen starts to spin. Search *Zerg rush* and a bunch of circles try to gobble up everything on the screen. You have to click each circle three times to get rid of it.

"Time to get off the computer," Mom says after a while.

"You're getting googly-eyed," Kai says. "Get it? *Google*-y-eyed!"

"What does *google* mean, anyway?" Mom asks.

"A google is a number," Ivan explains. "A big number. As you know, a million is a one with six zeroes, and a billion is a one with nine zeroes. Well, a google is a one with a *hundred* zeroes."

"It's so huge, there isn't a google of anything in the world," I say.

"Not even blades of grass?" Mom asks.

"No."

"Grains of sand?"

"Nope."

"Bread crumbs?"

"No."

"How about bread-crumb *crumbs?* Like, if you step on a crumb and it breaks into smaller crumbs."

"No."

"Atoms?"

"No."

Mom plants a kiss on my forehead. "Well, my love for you is bigger than a google."

I glance at Ivan. He just smiles. "My dad says stuff like that too."


*"Happy birthday to you*
*Happy birthday to you*
*Happy birthday, dear Filip*
*Happy birthday to you!"*

Dad puts the "birthday cake" in front of me—ten sticky baklava triangles, each one pierced with a birthday candle waving a flame.

"Make a wish!" Uncle Boris booms.

I fill my lungs, but I can't think of a thing to wish for. The candles slump into wax lumps. I finally blow.

The first nine go out easily, but the last one is stubborn.

I close in on the tenth candle flame and choke out my last puff of breath. *Whoo*. The flame vanishes. A plume of smoke swirls up from the black wick.

"What did you wish for?" Ivan asks.

"Don't tell," Kai advises. "It won't come true."

I say nothing.

My wish was the ultimate flake out—I wished to save my wish for later.

Uncle Mato starts singing "Happy Birthday" in Croatian. He has a sparkly voice to go with his sparkly smile. Normally everyone would join in, but today everyone listens, forks frozen halfway to their mouths. Uncle Mato's voice winds through the room.

*"Sretan rođendan ti*
*Sretan rođendan ti*
*Sretan rođendan, dragi Filip*
*Sretan rođendan ti!"*

When Uncle Mato finishes, Dad's face is red and shiny, and he makes a sound like he's choking on his baklava.

Dad's crying!

*Rap-rap.* Mrs. Zupan taps on our kitchen window with her fishing pole. Dad wipes his eyes on his sleeve.

Mrs. Zupan holds out a present. "Sorry I couldn't make it to your party, Filip, but I couldn't miss my Happy Joints exercise class."

"What is it?" I ask, reaching for the soft bundle.

But I know *exactly* what the present is. I tear away the thick, velvety wrapping paper, which I suspect is wallpaper. When Mrs. Zupan isn't cooking, she's pasting up wallpaper. Her apartment is getting smaller and smaller.

"Go on, open," Mrs. Zupan urges.

It's a...sweater vest!

Mrs. Zupan has knitted a sweater vest for every one of my last four birthdays. They're kind of...incredible. I never wear them out of the house. What I do is wear them at the computer, where she can see me. They're actually really warm. And I am growing out of last year's. This year's is maroon. With yellow diamonds. And a wide orange waistband.

"Nice!" Ivan says. "Put it on."

I pull the vest over my head. Mrs. Zupan sizes me up. "Handsome!"

"Would you like a piece of birthday baklava?" I ask.

"Yes, please. I worked up quite an appetite doing wrist roundabouts."

I extend a baklava across Apatosaurus Chasm, but halfway there the fork slides off the plate. Ivan and I stare as it tumbles down, flipping and glinting, getting smaller and smaller—then *shhkk*.

"Yes!"

We race down the building's echoing stairwell.

The fork is three centimeters deep in the dirt, tines first, a silver flag.

Ivan and I high-five each other. "Sick!"

"What's so exciting?"

A voice like fast water. Frances June D'Allaire. She's home from the pool, curly hair still wet, goggle imprints around her eyes, a perfume of chlorine. I breathe in deeply.

"A fork?" I squeak.

Ivan nudges me forward. He has this crazy idea that I have a crush on Frances June.

"We were just looking at how it landed—"

But Frances June isn't listening. She's staring at my vest.

"Oh. Mrs. Zupan—"

"I know all about it," Frances says. "She made me a swimsuit cover-up to keep me warm between races. It's pink and brown."

"It's Filip's birthday," Ivan blurts.

"Happy birthday!" Frances says. Then she turns and runs toward her building, where her mother is holding the door.

"You too!" I shout.

The door closes behind her.

"You *too*?" Ivan asks.

"Well, it could be her birthday," I mumble.

"Yes, it is statistically possible..." Ivan's voice trails off as he starts arranging numbers in his head. "Actually, more possible than you'd think..."

## Chapter Eight

Back at the apartment, Mrs. Zupan and Mom are eating their baklava and chatting. Mom has pulled a chair up to our kitchen window, Mrs. Zupan to hers.

I drop the fallen fork in the sink. When Mom and Mrs. Zupan hear the *clink*, they stop talking. Which is weird. Mom and Mrs. Zupan never stop talking. In fact, everything I know about adults is from listening in on their conversations.

Mom winks. "Nice vest. You look very noble."

Mom often says she would prefer a "noble" son to a "Nobel" son. She doesn't realize that I hope to be both noble *and* win the Nobel Prize.

Before I can answer, Dad, Uncle Boris, Kai and Uncle Mato swarm me. They grab me by my feet, my arms and my armpits and lift me in the air until my nose nearly touches the ceiling. Then they basically drop me on the hard kitchen floor.

*Bump!* Ow!

And up again. And down again.

*Bump!* Ow!

*Bump!* Ow!

*Bump!* Ow!

*Bump!* Ow!

*Bump!* Ow!

*Bump!* Ow!

*Bump!* Ow!

*Bump!* Ow!

*Bump!* Ow!

"And one for good luck!"

"No!" I scream.

"Oh, you want two for good luck?"

"Noooo!"

They give me three for good luck. Then they give me a present—a model kit of a turbine invented by Nikola Tesla. Ivan turns pale, he's so jealous.

While Uncle Boris and Kai get their coats on, Uncle Mato finds me in the living room and squats down. This worked when I was little, so we could be at eye level, but now that I'm taller it feels silly, since Uncle Mato has to look

up at me. "I may not be able to play soccer this week," he says.

"I've been replaced by a nurse?"

"Sort of. But you and I will hang out soon, okay?"

"Sure."

Uncle Mato gives me a long, serious hug.

"Why such a long, serious hug?" I ask.

Uncle Mato shrugs. My stomach clenches up like it's preparing for a punch. But Uncle Mato just kisses the top of my head. "Happy birthday, double-digit Filip."

Ivan and I work on my turbine model until Ivan's stomach growls and he heads to the kitchen for another piece of baklava.

When he returns, he's shaky.

"Did you break a glass or something?"

"No."

"What then?"

"Nothing."

"Uh, obviously something."

"Okay, something." Ivan gnaws his tongue. "Your parents are talking at the supper table."

"That's kind of normal."

"They're talking about—" Ivan swallows.

"Me? It's okay. I'm used to it."

"About your uncle Mato."

"About his new girlfriend?"

"He has one? Cool! It's about time too, hey? I mean—"

"What were they talking about?"

"Yeah, well, I guess, it seems, apparently, you know, like—"

"Spit it out."

"He has cancer."

*There's* the punch. But everything clicks into place too. Mom and Mrs. Zupan going quiet at the window. Dad crying when Uncle Mato sang. Mom at The Paprenjak, not wanting him to play soccer. How he met a nurse!

"I'll get your mom," Ivan says, backing out of the room.

A minute later Mom knocks at the door. She looks tired. "I didn't want you to find out now. Definitely not on your birthday. Not until we know how bad it is. Or how *not* bad it is. You know, he could be fine. The lump could be benign."

"Lump?"

"Near his bladder."

"Ugh."

"I'll be heading off," Ivan says. "Happy bir—well, not so happy, huh.

Thanks for having me over. I'm sorry about your uncle."

I give him my worst look.

"Hey," Mom says. "Don't dig a hole under the messenger."

"That's not the expression, Mom."

"It isn't Ivan's fault, Filip."

I look at Ivan. His nose is red. That means he's upset.

"Sorry," I say.

"It's okay. Let begonias be begonias, hey?"

It's our old joke.

From before I was ten.

From before Uncle Mato had cancer.


After Ivan's gone, I add the newest dinosaur to the shelf above my bed. I've got a full set now, one from every year at Bording Elementary: red *Triceratops* (kindergarten), green *Tyrannosaurus rex* (first grade), blue *Brachiosaurus* (second grade), orange *Pteranodon* (third grade), purple *Velociraptor* (fourth grade) and yellow *Stegosaurus* (fifth grade).

I name each one for someone in my family—Mom, Dad, Uncle Boris, me, Uncle Mato. Then I dig four Playmobil forest animals out of the Fry's Cocoa container to keep the dinosaurs company.

They are Mrs. Zupan (elk), Ivan (bear), Kai (deer) and Frances (fox). I arrange them around the candle with the saved wish.

I feed Hito the last of her birthday bloodworms.

Then I climb into bed.

Pull the blankets over my head.

And cry.

## Chapter Nine

When I wake up, nothing has changed.
Uncle Mato still has cancer.

"Is he going to die?" I ask Dad as we
eat leftover cheesy potato for breakfast.

"No."

"How do you know?"

"I hope and I pray."

"But you don't believe in God."

"I'm praying to everything. To this plate of cheesy potato even." Dad takes a bite.

"Come on, Dad."

"I am, Filip," Dad says, his mouth full. "I'm praying to that bird up there. I'm praying to the floor. *Let my baby brother be all right*." Dad swallows loudly and puts down his fork. "I can't eat."

"Does it make a difference? Praying?"

"It gives me something to do."

"He gets the results from the biopsy tomorrow," Mom says on her way past with a cup of coffee. "That's the cancer test. We'll know whether the lump is benign or malignant. They took a piece of it last week to examine. Malignant means it could still grow and cause problems. Benign means it is not harmful."

I study the windowsill. There's a long crack in the wood. With all my mental might I beam a message into the crack—*benign*.

The school's front door is as powerful as a drawbridge. Once I'm inside, I forget all about Uncle Mato. Well, a few times he comes to mind, and then my heart drops like a parachute with a hole torn in it. But then—*z-z-z-zup*—someone unzips a backpack, or—*wham!*—a door slams, and the page on my desk goes bright and calls to me, *Hey, get to work*.

The walk home is harder. My head buzzes. Is Uncle Mato in pain? Will the

lump be malignant? Will he die? Will we ever play soccer together again?

I want everything the way it was.

I'd even go back to being nine. Be nine. Benign.

At home I head straight for the computer. I say, "Okay, Google. *Cancer.*"

Up come the links—560 million results in less than a second.

Cancer is a problem with cells. We start out as one cell. A tiny squishy egg thing. The one cell divides into two cells. Then those two divide, making four. Those four divide, making eight. And so on until you're an adult with one hundred thousand billion cells. That's a one with fourteen zeroes after it.

The more divisions, the bigger the chance for things to go wrong. Cancer is when the divisions go weird—the cells take on strange shapes or sizes or colour. A chemical might have gotten into the system—through the water or air—and messed things up, or cigarette smoke, or maybe the cells are getting old, or maybe there's something genetic—a disease that runs in the family.

The main treatments are radiation, where a bunch of X-rays are beamed at the cancer, and chemotherapy, where a bunch of chemicals are injected into the blood. The treatments often make the patient sick. But you have to fight fire with fire.

*Rap-rap.* Mrs. Zupan is dangling a noodle. "Look what was in my lettuce!" she sings. Not a noodle. We transfer the worm across the Chasm carefully. It's our first exchange since the fork dropped.

"Hito will love it," I say. "Thank you."

But Hito isn't in her aquarium! She isn't hiding in her tinfoil pond. She's not in the pile of leaves. "Hitokage! Where are you?"

I move to take the lid off and poke around, but the lid already *is* off. Somehow it got knocked askew.

Hito has climbed out of her tank!

This is bad. A salamander can't go long without water. I ask Google for help. Turn down the heat, it tells me. Put wet towels on the floor—your salamander will be looking for moisture. Put food on the floor as a trap.

I ask Mrs. Zupan if she has more worms. She rustles through her head of lettuce. No luck. I run down to the yard and start digging.

Frances comes by, goggles swinging from her hand. "What are you doing?"

"I need worms. So I can find my salamander."

"I'm waiting for a ride to my swimming lesson. A pool carpool."

"Ha."

Frances digs around in a flower bed with me. "Did you have a good birthday?"

"Actually, it was lousy."

"It looked like you were having fun. With the fork. And the vest." She smiles her Frances smile, which normally makes everything else in the world disappear.

"Then I found out my uncle has cancer."

"Oh. That's terrible."

"I know."

"My grandma died of cancer."

"I hope Uncle Mato will live."

"I hoped my grandma would live."

The conversation isn't helping.

I find two worms tangled together in the dirt. "These should do," I say, standing.

"I got one too." Frances hands me a red wiggler, then wipes her hands on her jeans, leaving streaks of dirt. "I hope you find your salamander."

"You too," I say, heading toward our shoe box's front door.

I lay wet towels on the kitchen floor and scatter the worms around the apartment. But Hito doesn't show up. Finally I pour myself a bowl of cereal and sit at the computer again.

My hands hover over the keyboard as I think up a question that will solve everything. I'm like a pianist about to launch into a great song.

"Okay, Google," I say into the microphone. *"Will Uncle Mato be all right?"*

Hito! She scrambles across the keyboard and knocks my cereal over.

*Crash!* "Got you!"

I put her straight into the tinfoil pool. Eventually the pouch of skin above her heart rises and falls at its normal rate. Seventy-seven beats per minute. The same as mine.

I'm so relieved. I give her the red wiggler. "This worm is special," I tell her. "It's from Frances."

Back in the kitchen, the computer is rumbling weirdly. I grab the tea towel from the fridge handle and wipe off the milk and cereal splattered on the screen. I rub every inch of the glass.

*Rumble-rumble.* The computer isn't happy. *Shuzzle. Schazzle.*

Steam rises out of its vents, little tornadoes joining up in a big cloud.

*Shuzzuzzle. Schazzazzle.*

Then the rumbling stops. The steam clears.

"Hello."

A tiny woman is cross-legged on top of the computer! She has dark skin and curly hair and thick eyeglasses. She's wearing jeans, a green sweater and pink Converse runners.

"I didn't know Converse made such small sizes," I blurt.

"You have to do a special order." The little woman extends her hand. I pinch it gently between my finger and thumb.

"I am the Great Googlini. That makes me sound like a genie, but really I'm a librarian more than an Aladdin. I'm an archivist, information scientist, database technician. When people google questions, I'm the one who answers."

"You answer forty thousand searches a second?" I say. "Three billion searches a day?"

"Well, there are a few of us. But I *am* very busy." The Great Googlini reclips her barrette. "Which is why I can't stay long. I hope you'll understand. I just wanted to tell you that I can't answer your question. I can't tell you whether your uncle Mato is going to be all right or not. That's outside my scope."

"But you know everything."

"No. No one, not even I, can know the future. It's kind of a logical impossibility, since everything we do *now* shapes the future. The future can't *be* until it is made. It's like asking for a tapestry before anyone has woven it. Or for a cake before you've shopped for the ingredients. Anyway, would you really want to know? What if it was bad news? What would you do then?"

"I'd spend lots of time with him."

"You can do that if he's going to be okay too. What else?"

"I'd tell him how much I love him."

"You can tell him that anyway."

"Would it help?"

"Maybe."

"*Maybe*?"

"That's the best I can tell you. Anyway, I really have to go. The searches are pouring in." The Great Googlini glances at the wet towel on the kitchen floor. "That advice seemed dubious."

"Yeah. But I did find Hito. Frances helped too."

"Frances?"

"A kid I know."

"You're lucky to have friends."

"You're lucky to have so much informa—"

But the Great Googlini has already snapped her fingers and become steam. She funnels back through the computer vents.

I touch the computer's moist top. "Bye."

*Tap-tap.* Mrs. Zupan is at her window, waving a fire extinguisher. "Are you having a little fire?"

"No, no. Everything's fine."

"What was that cloud?"

"It was a—a sort of genie!"

I expect Mrs. Zupan to scold me for being silly. But instead she smiles the way she does when I put on Croatian music. "You have to be sly with genies," she says. "I've made you a walnut bread. Catch!"

A dense loaf sails across Apatosaurus Chasm. I hug it to me like a football. It feels like a normal loaf of bread, but inside, I know, there's a spiral, a whorl of cinnamon, like a surfer's tunnel wave.

There are wonders in the most normal-looking things.

And horrors. Such as rogue cells.

# Chapter Ten

*Malignant.* The ugliest word in the world. It is Dad's face crumpling as he holds the phone to his ear. Mom sucking in her breath like someone is yanking on her heart.

*Chemotherapy.* The second-ugliest word. Therapy with chemicals. Aren't chemicals what we're supposed to get away from? Isn't that why Paprenjak customers ask if the borscht is organic?

Mom dries her tears on the tea towel. "People bounce back," she says. She looks at me. "And Uncle Mato's tough. But he won't be able to play soccer for a while."

I remember what the Great Googlini said about spending time with Uncle Mato. "Can I video-chat with him instead?"

"That's a nice idea," Mom says. Then she gives me a hug, squeezing a little too tightly.

So on Wednesday, instead of playing soccer, Uncle Mato and I meet on my computer. He's in a hospital bed under a green sheet. Chemicals flow into his arm through a small hose from a plastic bag. He raises his iPad and gives me a tour of the room. All around him, other people are in beds under green sheets, getting chemotherapy too. Uncle Mato aims his iPad at a dark-haired nurse carefully removing a tube from someone's arm. She sticks her tongue out. "Mato! Stop!"

"That's her!" I say.

"Your uncle's doing great, Filip," Eileen says, putting her face close to the screen. "He'll be hanging out with you again in no time."

"In the meantime, Filip, you can do me a favor," Uncle Mato says. "I'd like you to go to the park and kick the ball around, even though I'm not with you. It would make me feel better. Or go for a bike ride and feel the wind in your face, which is what I'd like to do."

A machine beeps, and Eileen fiddles with the tube feeding chemicals into Uncle Mato's arm.

"Are you scared, Uncle Mato?"

"Part of me is terrified." Uncle Mato holds up his little finger. "This part. But the rest of me is hopeful."

"You've just got to be patient," Eileen says.

"I'm *your* patient," Uncle Mato jokes. "But yeah, I'm patient." He points to his earlobe. "Except for this part. This part of me is very impatient."

When we hang up, I jump on my bike and head to Ivan's. Ivan doesn't like biking. Or walking. Or any kind of sport. But when I tell him about Uncle Mato, he wants to help. We pump up his bike tires and oil his bike chain and head to the park.

"Feel that wind!" I shout.

"It isn't wind," Ivan says. "It's friction."

At the park we try to repeat Uncle Mato's famous ricochet goal. If we get it,

I tell myself, Uncle Mato will be all right. But after a hundred tries, we surrender and pedal home in the dark.

Frances is in front of her building, a jacket over her swimsuit, towel over her shoulders. I squeeze my brakes. "My uncle's getting chemotherapy."

"Grandma got that too. It made her sick. And really tired. And it didn't help."

Frances sure doesn't help me feel better. Ivan said the right thing. What did he say? Right. He said *sorry*.

"I'm sorry," I say to Frances. "That must have been sad."

Her shoulders relax. It's like I turned a key or something. "It's just so weird that I'll never eat her cookies again," she says. "Our phone still speed-dials her apartment. I tried it. I thought the phone would just ring and ring. But someone answered. I had to say sorry, that I'd gotten the wrong number. And the person was rude, like *Don't call here again.* Anyway, Grandma was old. Your uncle Mato isn't old, though, right? Not *old* old. He could get over it. I hope he will."

"Hey, could you—no, forget it."

"What?"

"Could you swim a length at the pool for him? He asked me to do fun stuff, like bike around, since he can't."

"Sure. I'll swim the butterfly for him. That's the toughest, most satisfying stroke."

Before bed, I add a Playmobil dog to the circle of animals on the shelf. I name it Eileen. Then I place the *Stegosaurus*— Uncle Mato—right in the center of the circle, so it's like the others are protecting him. Then I stick the birthday candle with the saved wish into a thick slice of walnut loaf and call Mom to light it. I explain that I've still got a wish to make.

"Please, let Uncle Mato get better," I say as I blow out the candle. "And then he and Eileen get married."

# Chapter Eleven

Ivan and I go trick-or-treating together. Ivan is dressed as Frankenstein's monster, which works because he's so tall and his head is kind of square. I'm Harry Potter. Again. I couldn't think up another costume. I just don't care that much this year.

Uncle Mato usually takes me out. He just wears his pajamas and a top hat, and paints blood dripping from his mouth. These days, Uncle Mato looks frightening *without* a costume. He has lost weight, and his face is very white except for dark circles under his eyes. The weirdest thing is, he has lost his hair. Including his thick eyebrow.

But it's supposed to grow back. He finished his chemotherapy five days ago, and soon they'll take a picture with MRI—magnetic resonance imaging. Magnetic-field waves and sound waves will bounce around and map his insides. The MRI will show if the lump is shrinking.

While we're trick-or-treating, Ivan and I run into Frances. She's dressed up as Penny Oleksiak, the Olympic swimmer, with a gold medal around her neck. It's actually a chocolate coin on a string. Under a huge towel, to keep her warm, Frances is wearing her swimsuit and goggles and swim cap, and she's written a competitor's number on her leg in grease paint.

She points to a house across the street that has no Halloween decorations, just a light over the front step. "I hear they're giving away toothbrushes!"

"Now that's really scary," Ivan says.

"I've swum a length for Uncle Mato every practice," Frances tells me. "And I've started to swim a length for my grandma too. I know she's not coming back—but I like thinking about her."

"Mrs. Zupan makes a stew that her grandma used to make. It makes her cry. Can you imagine how old that recipe is?"

Frances smiles. "My grandma made the best chocolate-chip cookies. They

had something chewy in them. I'd trade all the candy in this bag for just one."

"Filip Horvat to the office, please."

What did I do? It's not my birthday.

"Your mother called," Principal Jansen explains. "With a message for you. She said she didn't want you to worry for another minute." Principal Jansen rustles around for a piece of paper on her desk. "*The lump has shrunk,*" she reads. "*It has shrunk to nothing.*"

I float back to class.

Uncle Mato's cancer has been stopped in its evil tracks!

For the first time in months, Uncle Mato is at The Paprenjak. With the soccer ball.

And his eyebrow! Well, most of his eyebrow. It's a little thinner than before and broken in two. In fact, he looks great! He jumps up when I come in and holds me high in the air.

"Careful!" Mom says.

Uncle Mato and I laugh.

Everything's like normal. I even ask The Question while we walk to the field. "Do you have a girlfriend?"

"I do," Uncle Mato answers, smiling. "She's funny and smart and kind, and I'm very lucky."

"*Lucky*? You had cancer!"

"Yeah. Strange, isn't it? Cancer is lousy. But it would have been far worse without Boris and Kai and your dad and mom bringing meals, driving me to the hospital for chemo treatments, helping keep my apartment clean. And you telling me about the real world, the unsick world—that made it easier."

"That helped?"

I think of Dad talking to his cheesy potatoes and my postponed birthday wish, and Mom crossing her fingers when the call came through and the lump was malignant. That stuff made *us* feel better. But it probably didn't help Uncle Mato much.

"Yes. It helped. It meant I didn't have a chance to get afraid, and I was never too uncomfortable. I was never—alone."

Uncle Mato drop-kicks the ball.

The ball hits the tree—two birds flap out.

The ball bounces off the telephone pole.

And—goal!

Uncle Mato and I hit the ground laughing. We lie there until the world quiets.

"Good riddance, lump!" I shout at the sky.

"*Zbogom*!" Uncle Mato yells, shaking his fist. "*Nemojte se vratiti.*"

"Yeah! Don't ever come back."

# Chapter Twelve

Frances's mom is lugging groceries from the car. I ask if I can help. Mrs. D'Allaire points to a bag of flour the size of a toddler. "If you could lug that to the door, I would be grateful."

There's a small tear in the bag, so when I pick it up, a puff of flour wheezes out. It reminds me of the Great Googlini coming out of the computer.

"Mrs. D'Allaire?"

"Yes?"

"What kind of cookies did Frances's grandmother always bake?"

Mrs. D'Allaire suddenly looks windblown. "Yes, my mom was a great baker. Her coconut–chocolate-chip cookies were Frances's favorite."

"Coconut–chocolate-chip."

"Yes."

I put the groceries inside the door of her building. I take a quick breath, like I'm about to jump into cold water. "I'm sorry your mom died."

It doesn't come out as loudly as I meant it to, but Mrs. D'Allaire hears me. I know, because she gives me that look Mom gives me right before she starts talking about how I should win the "noble prize."

When I get home, I tap out four words in the Google search bar.

*Uncle Mato is okay.*

I stare at the top of the computer hopefully. Nothing.

I type again. *Uncle Mato is okay!*

Nothing. No steam. No rumbling. I think back to when Hito spilled my cereal. I get the tea towel and rub the screen.

*Rumble. Shuzzle. Shazzle.* Steam curls out of the top of the computer.

*Poof!* This time, instead of Converse runners, the Great Googlini is wearing

Birkenstocks. "It's hot today. Tons of activity. Hey, that's good news about your uncle. What made him better?"

"Medicine, mostly. And people keeping him company. I understand why you couldn't answer my question before."

"From what I have figured out, some questions just can't be answered. But people still need to ask them. You've met an unhappy mystery, Filip. Still, from what I can tell from the questions people ask, most mysteries in this world are happy ones."

"I'm ready for one of those."

The Great Googlini adjusts her sandal buckle. "I'd better get back to work. You might be interested in a new study. A scientist has proposed that dinosaurs were warm-blooded!"

"I'll look it up," I say as the Great Googlini dissolves to mist and twirls back through the computer vents.

First, though, I look up the recipe for coconut–chocolate-chip cookies.

We don't have all the ingredients, but Mrs. Zupan hands an egg and a bag of coconut across the gap. She teaches me how to cream butter and sugar. Basically, you mash the two with the back of the wooden spoon.

After supper I take the stairwell steps two at a time.

I feel light as air. Happy about Uncle Mato and happy to be on my way to Frances's!

Outside, the sky is salted with stars.

My uncles don't see so many stars in the city. There's too much light from the office buildings and streetlights.

You need a little darkness to see the stars.

The cookie tin is warm and heavy in my hands as I map Ursa Major and the Belt of Orion.

It's a school night in Bording, British Columbia. I don't feel bored at all.

# Acknowledgments

Thank you very much to Dragan, who cast a knowledgeable Croatian eye on this novel, confirming—or laughing at—its references to Croatian food and culture. And love always to my dear son, Ezra, who overheard with me a woman on the Paris Metro telling a friend she was "a master googler" who could find anything on the Internet. His trip to the Pompidou was delayed as I squatted on a curb, scribbling the notes that became this book. Thanks too to Hazel and Alden, who support and encourage their mom always. And thank you to Andrew, without whom—and without Google—I would not have had the life-changing joy of meeting. Thanks to ever-inspiring friends Pam, Leslie, John, Julie, Andrea, Lesley, Bruce, Amaya, Amanda and Liz McG. And to my generous, inventive editor, Liz Kemp.

*Sara Cassidy* is a poet and journalist and the author of nine books for young readers, including *Slick* and *Skylark*. Her books have been selected for the Junior Library Guild, and she has been a finalist for the Kirkus Children's Literature Prize, the Chocolate Lily Award and the Bolen Books Children's Book Prize. Sara has taught at Camosun College and Royal Roads University. For more information, visit saracassidywriter.com.